A Horse's Best Friend

Winnie
The Early Years

A Horse's Best Friend

Dandi Daley Mackall

illustrated by Phyllis Harris

TYNDALE
KIDS

Tyndale House Publishers, Inc.
Carol Stream, IL

Visit Tyndale's website for kids at www.tyndale.com/kids.

Visit Dandi Daley Mackall online at www.dandibooks.com.

TYNDALE is a registered trademark of Tyndale House Publishers, Inc. The Tyndale Kids logo is a trademark of Tyndale House Publishers, Inc.

A Horse's Best Friend

Designed by Jacqueline L. Nuñez

Edited by Sarah Rubio

For manufacturing information regarding this product, please call 1-800-323-9400.

For information about special discounts for bulk purchases, please contact Tyndale House Publishers at csresponse@tyndale.com, or call 1-800-323-9400.

Library of Congress Cataloging-in-Publication Data

Names: Mackall, Dandi Daley, author. | Harris, Phyllis, date- illustrator.
Title: A horse's best friend / Dandi Daley Mackall ; illustrations by Phyllis Harris.
Description: Carol Stream, Illinois : Tyndale Kids, Tyndale House Publishers, Inc., [2018]
  | Series: Winnie: the early years | Summary: Eight-year-old Winnie is torn between being
  a good friend to her old horse, Chief, and unpopular friend, Simon, and wrangling an
  invitation to mean girl Tamson's birthday sleepover.
Identifiers: LCCN 2018027391 | ISBN 9781496432841 (sc)
Subjects: | CYAC: Christian life—Fiction. | Friendship—Fiction. | Popularity—Fiction.
  | Horses—Fiction. | Ranch life—Wyoming—Fiction. | Wyoming—Fiction.
Classification: LCC PZ7.M1905 Hs 2018 | DDC [Fic]—dc23 LC record available at https://
  lccn.loc.gov/2018027391

Printed in the United States of America

24	23	22	21	20	19	18
7	6	5	4	3	2	1

For Cassie, who—like her grandmother—loves horses

There are "friends" who pretend to be friends, but there is a friend who sticks closer than a brother.

PROVERBS 18:24

Contents

Chapter 1

Mustang Madness

"Where are they?" I ask, trying not to whine. And failing.

Mom and I are lying on our bellies behind some bushes. We've been waiting over an hour to see Mustangs. Wind rips across the hillside. Shadows move on the purple mountains.

"Be patient, Winnie," Mom says. "It was your idea to come with me."

Every year Mom comes here to watch wild horses. And every year I beg to come along. This is the first year she's said okay. We drove our trailer because sometimes Mom brings back a horse to gentle. She trains it, then sells it. The money goes to the wild horse refuge in Laramie.

So far, we've seen only three deer and an antelope. No Mustangs. And now I can't get that song out of my head: *Home, home on the range, where the deer and the antelope play . . .*

"So, Winnie, how are you getting along at school?" Mom asks.

Now I get it. Mom let me tag along because she already knows the answer to her question: I'm *not* getting along at school.

"Okay," I mutter.

She waits me out. Mom is the most patient human in the world. She can train any horse because she doesn't rush or lose her temper. She's the best horse gentler in Wyoming. And she's pretty good with daughters, too.

Finally, I give in. "Well, maybe not so great." Tamson invited all of the popular girls in my class for a sleepover birthday party. Not me. No surprise. At recess, Tamson tells us what to play. Lately, it's jail tag. I'm not invited to do that either, so I swing or sit by myself—jail without the tag.

I'd do anything to be invited to Tamson's sleepover.

Mom stares at the crest of the hill. "What's not great?" she asks.

Tamson's face pops into my mind. "Mom, did you ever have a bossy girl in your class who ruined everything?"

Mom sighs. "I did. Stephanie. That girl thought she owned the school. I think she had parties just to leave me out."

I can't believe this. Everybody likes my mom. "What did you do?"

"I let her boss me around for almost a whole year because I wanted her to like me. Then I decided to ignore her. As soon as I did, I got to know Laurie."

Laurie is my mom's best friend. "But how did—"

"Shh!" Mom whispers. "They're coming. Feel it?"

"I don't feel any—" I stop. I *do* feel it. The ground shakes. The sound of hooves grows louder. I peek.

At the top of the hill, two horses rush at each other. The bay rears and strikes a hoof to the black stallion's neck. The black rears and twists, then bites the bay's belly.

"Mom!" I cry. "Stop them!"

"It's all right," she says. "The black stallion is keeping the younger stallion in line."

In seconds, the bay drops back to the other horses, who were watching from the top of the hill. The black stallion arches his neck and whinnies his victory. He rears. When his hooves strike the ground, he breaks into a gallop.

More horses appear over the hill.
A Buckskin. A paint. A pinto. A dozen bays.
They follow the stallion at high speed. The
whole herd thunders down the hill . . .
And straight at us.

Chapter 2

The Herd Nerd

I watch, frozen to my spot, as the herd of wild horses gallops toward us. I shut my eyes and pray. That's what my sister, Lizzy, would do. "God, don't let us be stomped to death!"

Mom laughs. "We're fine, Winnie. They're racing to that stream in the valley. That's why I always start out here. Sooner or later, the horses will need to drink."

Mustangs run past us to the stream. They take long drinks, side by side, like they're all buddies. They are beautiful. Four foals spread their forelegs and lower their heads to nose the water.

Something rises inside me. Suddenly, I'm so grateful to be here with Mom.

"I thought Mustangs were small and scraggly," I tell Mom.

"Some are. These are mixed. Wild horses were brought here from Spain. *Mustang* comes from a Spanish word that means 'stray horse.' See that Buckskin mare? She's the boss."

"Wait. I thought the black stallion was boss."

"It's his herd, all right," Mom explains. "But *she's* the boss."

I watch "the boss." She shoves a young stallion away and lets one of the foals in. When another mare tries to come up to the water, the Buckskin bucks. She really is the boss.

"That mare reminds me of Tamson," I mutter to myself.

"Tamson?" Mom asks. "Tamson Fry?"

When I nod, Mom laughs so loud a couple of horses look our way. But they must have decided we're no threat. They go back to drinking. "I should have known!" Mom says. "My Stephanie is Tamson's mom. In the wild, the filly of a herd's bossy mare usually becomes the bossy mare when she's old enough. Imagine that."

I watch, and I imagine. I can almost see Tamson pushing and shoving horses into line.

The bossy mare whinnies. I think she's telling the herd it's time to leave. She leads them to a grassy patch up the hill. They graze together.

Except one horse stays by the stream. She looks like I thought Mustangs would—scraggly. Her short mane stands up like a rooster's comb. She's gray with specks of brown, like big freckles.

When she tries to catch up with the herd, the Buckskin turns on her, ears back, teeth showing.

The little Mustang stops. She hangs her head.

"That's just mean!" I say.

"It happens," Mom says. "Sometimes, for whatever reason, a bossy mare decides a certain horse doesn't fit in. Poor little thing. She's the herd nerd."

Note to self: I know exactly how that Mustang feels.

Chapter 3

The Home Herd

"You're back!" Lizzy squeals when Mom and I pull up with the trailer. My sister is a year younger than me, except for one day a year (her birthday) when we're the same age. But she's taller. And prettier. And nicer. "Did you get a horse?"

Mom parks by the barn. I hop out and open the tailgate so Mom can back out our new horse.

"I'm sure this horse is very smart. But her

coat is not a work of art." The rhyme, as always, comes from our friend Simon. We call
him Rhymin' Simon at school. He and his
twin, Austin, are in my class.

Mom and I agreed that we had to rescue the
outcast Mustang.

"What's her name?" Lizzy asks, keeping her

distance. She is as scared of horses as I am of her spiders and lizards.

"Rainbow," Mom answers.

"Hobo," I answer at the same time.

Simon says, "She looks kind of plucky. So how about Lucky?"

Lizzy claps her hands. "I love it!"

"Lucky it is," Mom agrees.

"Lucky?" I ask. "Really? Nobody in the herd wanted her there."

"Then we'll have to make sure Lucky feels wanted here," Mom says.

Mom tries to lead Lucky into the barn. But Lucky won't go peacefully. She rears. She jerks the lead rope. She plants her legs and won't move.

Lizzy shouts, "Mom, what's wrong?"

Rhymin' Simon adds, "Lucky's strong."

I start toward Mom, but she shakes her head. She doesn't want my help.

Mom tries calming the horse by scratching her neck. Her fingers move to the top of Lucky's shoulder: the withers.

Lucky stops struggling.

Mom keeps scratching and leads Lucky away from the barn.

I jog ahead and open the pasture gate.

Mom unsnaps the lead rope and turns Lucky into the pasture.

Four horses are grazing together in the pasture. One is Austin's champion Thoroughbred, Royal Princess. The remaining three belong to some of Mom's other clients. Buttermilk, Mom's Buckskin Quarter Horse, must be in the barn.

Then there's old Chief, our farm horse. The big gelding came with the ranch. He's scratching his rump on an apple tree.

Lucky, ears back in anger or fear, steps past Chief. The Mustang bucks in Chief's direction. Chief doesn't seem to care.

Lucky's ears prick forward when she sees the other horses. She whinnies.

The four horses stop grazing. Their heads bob up as if they're on the same puppet string.

Only Princess returns a whinny. But it sounds more like a threat than a welcome.

"Uh-oh," Mom says.

"What?" Lizzy demands. She and Simon are hanging over the gate. Mom and I are inside the pasture.

I know why Mom is worried. "Princess is the boss of her little herd," I explain. "She's not going to like Lucky."

"Why not?" Lizzy asks. "I think Lucky's cute."

Princess does not agree. Ears flat back, neck arched, she charges. Her herd follows.

I smell Lucky's fear. The fuzz on her back stands up. Her tail swishes fast.

Princess leads the pack. They're coming to fight.

Closer and closer.

My heart is pounding. I shoot up a prayer, even though I can't form words in my head. I look from Lizzy and Simon to Mom, to Chief.

"Somebody, do something!" I cry.

Chapter 4

Odd Girl Out

Mom throws herself in front of the charging Princess.

Lizzy screams.

"Mom!" I shout. She's going to end up squished between Princess and Lucky.

Mom holds up both hands, fingers spread. She stares at Princess. "No! Back!"

The other horses drop to a walk. Princess slows down but keeps coming.

"Winnie," Mom says, like we're just talking about the weather. "Go to the barn and rattle the feed bin."

I race to the barn and slap the nearest feed bin. I shake the oats inside. I whistle the way I do when I feed the horses.

I hear the *thump thump* of hooves before I see the horses. Princess is in the lead. I scoop oats and dump them into her stall feeder. She runs in. I feed the other horses in their stalls.

Mom walks in. "Not exactly a warm welcome."

"It's all Princess's fault," I say.

Note to self: there's a Tamson in every crowd.

The next day, instead of taking the bus to school, Lizzy and I accept Dad's offer to drop us off on his way to work. Last night I couldn't stop thinking about Tamson and her sleepover. Then I had a thought. Maybe Tamson, or Tamson's mother, just forgot to send me an invitation to her party.

"Okay, girls." Dad has the invention gleam in his eye. "How about a pocket hat?"

I don't get it, but Lizzy says, "Sounds great, Dad!"

Dad explains. "I'd always have my keys there. You could keep pencils. Notepads. Candy! Easy to make. Low cost."

"Dad, you missed our turn." I sigh.

Out the window, I see Simon. He's waving. Lizzy waves back.

Miss Pento, our teacher, hasn't started teaching yet when I slide into my seat in the back row. Tamson is turned around in her seat. She's talking to Landri about the party.

"And movies!" Tamson says. "And popcorn. Mom's making brownies with frosting."

I lean over so I can hear.

"Hi, Winnie," Landri says. She's part of the popular group. But Landri is nice. She probably doesn't know Tamson left me out.

"What do you want, Winnie?" Tamson snaps.

"Nothing." I fake a laugh. "The party sounds fun."

"It will be," Tamson says.

Simon sits in front of me. He turns around. "When's our class trip to Lizzy's farm? Bugs and lizards will do no harm."

Before I can answer, Tamson makes a face. "Ew! Do we have to go?"

Note to self: why can't Lizzy play with dolls instead of lizards?

Chapter 5

Don't Bug Me!

Miss Pento prances to the front of the class. Her blonde ponytail swishes. If she were a horse, she'd be a spirited Welsh Pony.

"In honor of National Science Week," Miss Pento begins, "we'll be learning about animals. Today, Simon is showing us his bug collection."

Groans rise from the class as Simon walks to the front.

From the first row, Austin, Simon's twin, whispers to Seth and cracks up laughing.

Seth smiles but doesn't laugh. He's a whole lot nicer than Austin.

Simon sets two lunch boxes on the teacher's desk. "These are bugs. I'm their coach. The toughest bug is this cockroach." He explains that one species of cockroach can live in the Arctic and another would be just fine buried in desert sands.

"Please put it back, Simon," Miss Pento says.

Simon takes out a green caterpillar. "These guys make me think of God. How they change is very odd."

"Like Simon," Tamson whispers, loud enough for us to hear.

Everyone around her giggles. She looks at me, waiting.

I don't exactly laugh. But I smile.

Tamson smiles back.

Simon rhymes his way through both lunch boxes. He shows us a singing cricket named Jimmy and explains that only the boy crickets sing. They do it to get girl crickets. He takes out a queen ant and points out that there's no "king ant."

He has a girl spider who can eat 25 boy spiders a day.

"And now, I've saved the best for last! This roly-poly isn't fast."

"Maybe that *roly-poly* is your real twin," Austin shouts.

Simon isn't fat. But he's not as thin as Austin. The whole class laughs.

When Tamson turns to see if I'm joining in, I laugh too. But only on the outside.

Simon keeps going like he hasn't heard

Austin. He shows us that his "pill bug" or "potato bug" isn't round now. "But when I touch it, it rolls into a ball. See how the roly-poly rolls so small?" He moves to show Miss Pento.

But his arm bumps a lunch box.

The lunch box crashes to the floor.

Bugs crawl everywhere. Girls scream. Boys shriek.

Miss Pento jumps onto her desk. One of her shoes flies off.

Simon drops to his knees. He herds the bugs into his lunch box. "Never fear! Bugs all here."

Miss Pento gets the class to stop screaming and settle down. Our teacher gracefully steps from her desk to her chair to the floor. "That was quite . . . interesting, Simon. Thank you."

Simon is staring into his lunch box. I see him silently counting bugs. He looks to the floor, then back to his lunch box.

And I know. He's lost one of his bugs.

Miss Pento picks up her shoe and keeps talking. "Tomorrow we take the bus to the Willis Wyoming Ranch for our field trip. Winnie's sister, Lizzy, has agreed to show us her lizard collection."

Tamson rolls her eyes at Landri.

I stare at my desk. For the millionth time, I tell God how much I want to go to Tamson's sleepover. But what if Tamson thinks lizards are creepy? And my sister is creepier? And that makes me—

"Aaaarg!" Miss Pento screams. She kicks off her shoe. The roly-poly, now rolled into a black ball, sails out of her shoe through the air. It heads straight for Austin.

Note to self: the lost has been found.

Chapter 6

Friendship

Something has changed.

At recess, Tamson asks me to play jail tag.
She puts me on the other team. And everybody except Simon plays. But still.

On the bus, I head for my seat in the back.

But Tamson stops me. "Sit by us." She
points to the seat in front of her.

I obey, sitting next to Myra, one of the popular kids.

We talk together. I almost feel like one of them. Tamson makes a few jokes about Simon's bug show. I laugh along. First I make sure Simon is in the back, where I usually sit. He can't hear us.

We're almost to my stop.

Tamson looks at me like she's never seen me before. "Winnie, you're all right."

Myra, Landri, and the others nod.

"Do you have anything going on Friday night?" Tamson asks.

Friday night? That's her birthday. Her sleepover. "No!" I almost shout.

The bus jerks to a stop. My stop.

Lizzy and Simon get off. "Winnie!" Lizzy shouts. "Our stop."

I stand. I want Tamson to say it. I know she's about to invite me to her party.

"Out!" yells Mr. Ted, our bus driver.

I move to the aisle. Then I look back at Tamson.

She's not looking at me. She's talking to the popular girls.

I jump out as the bus doors close behind me.

As soon as I get home, I run to the pasture to look for Chief. I need him to help me figure out what's going on.

I spot Lucky at one end of the pasture and Princess's tiny herd on the other.

Why can't they be friends? I wonder this, but I'm saying it to God too. *Jesus was friends with everybody.* God already knows that. But it feels good to talk to him about it.

Chief nickers when he sees me. I sit on the fence, and the big plow horse comes and puts his head in my lap. I scratch his cheeks, and he closes his eyes.

"Chief," I begin. "I think I'm starting to make friends with the coolest kids in our class. I really want to go to Tamson's sleepover."

Chief's soft breathing calms me.

I lean down and blow into his nostril. He blows back. This is how horses greet friends. "You're a good friend, Chief."

Simon flashes through my mind. I hope he didn't hear me on the bus. "I wasn't a very good friend today. It's hard sometimes." I stroke Chief under his mane. "You never graze with the other horses. Does that bother you?"

Chief groans with happiness from being scratched. He doesn't seem bothered.

"Winnie!" Mom calls from the house. "Homework."

I join Mom and Lizzy inside. "How did Lucky get along today?" I ask.

"I'd like to work her in the round pen." Mom sets down a glass of milk for me. "But Lucky needs to think of me as a friend first. And right now, I just don't have the time I need to earn her friendship."

Mom can always get horses to trust her. It's like she can read their minds. And hearts. But she insists on taking her time with them.

"How about the other horses?" I ask.

Mom sighs. "No friends there, I'm afraid. Not yet anyway."

Note to self: when did friendship get so hard?

Chapter 7

Phooey on Field Trips

Next morning, Simon boards the field trip bus with me as if we're going to sit together as usual.

But Tamson waves me over.

"I'm sitting up here today," I tell Simon. This has to be the day Tamson invites me to her party. The sleepover is tomorrow.

"I am not looking forward to this field trip," Tamson gripes. "Bugs and lizards?"

"Yeah," I say, like I agree. "But think about it. We could be having a science test instead."

"Or a math test," Myra adds.

Tamson leans forward. "Or another bug disaster with Rhymin' Simon."

My face laughs along with them, but not my heart.

The closer we get to my ranch, the more nervous I get. My stomach feels like Lizzy's lizards are in there and looking for a way out.

I love our ranch, and I wouldn't want to live anywhere else. But as we pile out of the bus, I see things like Tamson and the others might. Our barn could use a new roof. So could our house. The porch sags. Dad forgot to mow the grass.

Tamson jogs to catch up with Austin. I jog after her.

"Austin!" Tamson calls. "Show us your horse."

We've been training Princess—and Austin—to ride for a few weeks. Princess is coming along nicely. Austin, not so much. If he listened to Mom like his horse does, everything would be great.

"You want to know which horse is mine?" Austin asks. "That's easy!" He leads us to the gate and points out his Thoroughbred mare. "Mine is the expensive one."

Princess and her herd, including Mom's Buckskin, continue to graze. But for the first time, Chief and Lucky are grazing together. Chief is so big, and Lucky is so little. They make an odd pair.

"Whose are those ugly horses?" Tamson points out Chief and Lucky and laughs.

Austin shrugs. "I've never seen that

little one before. I would have remembered. Yuck!"

"It's a wild horse, a Mustang we caught. We'll sell it as soon as we're done training it," I explain quickly.

"You think somebody will buy *that?*" Austin asks. "The big ugly one is Winnie's horse." Tamson turns and wrinkles her nose like I smell bad. "*That's* your horse?"

"Not really," I say. "Old Chief came with the ranch. We didn't have a choice. We had to keep him." Right away, I feel bad. *I'm sorry, God.* I'll tell Chief I'm sorry later.

Miss Pento calls us over to Lizzy's lizard farm. Lizzy has set out horse blankets for us to sit on.

Tamson frowns down at the green saddle blanket Mom used on Buttermilk when she competed in barrel races. "Isn't there anywhere else to sit? I don't want to smell like a horse."

Myra jumps up from the Navajo blanket spread out next to the green one. "Ooh! I didn't think of that."

"*I'm* sure not sitting on those things," Austin says.

Lizzy smiles at them, although I don't know how she can. I feel like running into the house and hiding under my bed. "You're welcome to stand if you like. But all of our saddle blankets have been washed. I think you'll discover they're soft as clouds."

Austin and Tamson take a seat. But they make sure we know they're unhappy about it. Everybody else sits down too.

Lizzy takes her first lizard from its cage. She holds it in front of her, showing it to her audience. When she speaks, her voice is clear and bright, like she's just talking to Simon or me. My voice, which always sounds a little hoarse, would be shaking like a horse's tail in fly season.

"Ladies and gentlemen," Lizzy begins, "I would like you all to meet one of my favorite lizards. His name is Bug. Now, a lot of people

call this fine creature a Horned Toad. But I assure you that Bug is a Horned Lizard. You may not know this, but the Horned Lizard is the official state reptile of Wyoming."

Somebody says, "Wow! I didn't know that." Everybody is listening.

Lizzy shows us her Red-Lipped Plateau Lizard and her Great Plains Earless. Her smile is so real and friendly. I look around and see everyone smiling back, even Tamson.

"Isn't it amazing that God would take time to create 5,600 species of lizards?" Lizzy asks. "God and Jesus must love lizards as much as I do!"

If I said something like that, the popular kids would stare or laugh at me. But when Lizzy says it, kids nod and agree. Everybody likes Lizzy. She's popular, and she doesn't even try.

I love my sister more than anybody, but I wish this field trip would be over.

Chapter 8

To Be . . . or Not to Be . . . a Friend

After the lizard show, Miss Pento chats with
Mom. We kids check out the rest of Lizzy's
lizards.

Simon says, "You've made these cages into
home. No wonder lizards no more roam."

"Thanks, Simon," Lizzy says. "I should have
told your class how much help you've been
with the lizards."

"Simon!" Tamson shouts. She points at a cage. "This lizard looks just like you."

Lizzy moves between Tamson and Simon. "They're both handsome," she says. "Simon was a big help collecting these lizards. I don't think anyone else could have found a Great Plains Earless around here. And he found it twice!"

"That's because my brother has so much in common with lizards," Austin says.

Tamson adds, "And roly-polies!" She laughs harder than everybody else put together.

I don't laugh. But I don't speak up for Simon either.

Simon shuffles away. No rhyme this time.

I watch as he wanders off toward the pasture. Something about the way his shoulders slump and his head hangs down reminds me of Lucky when the Mustang herd ran off and left her alone.

In my mind, I ask God to do something to make Simon feel better. But I know I should do something too.

While my classmates hover around the lizard village and ask Lizzy questions, I walk toward the pasture. But I stop when I get close. I don't think Simon sees me.

Simon climbs the fence and sits on the top rung. He wipes his glasses on his sleeve.

Chief walks up and lays his head on Simon's lap.

Simon jerks, and I'm afraid he'll fall. But he catches himself. Then he pats Chief on the head.

I know Chief doesn't like that kind of a pat. But he stays there anyway.

Chief is a way better friend than I am.

I climb up and sit beside Simon. He smiles at me, and I feel rotten.

"Chief is my best friend." I sigh. "Sometimes it feels like he's my only friend."

Simon frowns at me. "Really?"

"Really." I reach over and scratch Chief's cheek. "I wish Chief could come to school with me."

"And on field trips?" Simon asks. I wait, but he still isn't rhyming.

"Everywhere."

We climb down, and I look back to see Princess leading her herd to the barn. Lucky tries to follow, but Princess shuts her out.

Chief trots into the pasture toward Lucky.

"Where's Chief going?" Simon asks.

"Watch," I tell him, knowing what's coming. "Good ol' Chief is trotting to the rescue."

Sure enough, Chief trots up behind Princess, positioning himself between Princess and Lucky. Princess snorts. Then she seems to decide the two "ugly" horses, as Tamson called them, aren't worth the trouble. She and her herd drift away and leave Lucky alone.

At least Lucky has a real friend.

The field trip has taken all day, so Miss Pento tells Mom that Lizzy and I don't have to ride the bus back to school. We'd just get there and have to turn around and ride the bus home again.

Once everybody is gone, I can't shake my bad feeling about everything that's happened today. I know I let Simon down. And Lizzy. And even Chief.

I need to do what I always do when I can't make sense of things. I need to go for a ride.

Chief is always easy to catch. I brush him. Then I bridle him with a snaffle bit. But Chief and I don't need a saddle.

"Come on, my friend," I whisper as I open the gate and lead him through. Already, the scent of horse and the feel of his coat have me breathing more easily. "Let's head for the woods, Chief."

I close the gate and lead Chief outside. Then I guide him up next to the fence so I can get on.

He's way too big for me to jump on bareback.
Chief stands still while I climb to the top rung
and then onto his back. "Good boy. Ready?"

Even though Chief is ten years older than
any other horse on the ranch, his gathered
muscles and high head let me know he's as
ready for a ride as I am. I barely squeeze with
my thighs, and he's off at a fast pace.

I look between his ears to the woods, and
Chief senses that's where I want to go. He
enters the trail that we've made with our
many rides here. I don't have to guide Chief.
He knows me. I duck a low-hanging branch.
Then I let my head stay resting on Chief's
broad neck. His mane strokes my cheek, and
the horsey smell of him mingles with the
earthy scent of the woods.

I hug Chief, stretching my arms around
his neck as far as they'll go. I close my eyes

and let my body rock with his steady beat as if we're one creature. I can almost imagine we are.

"Thanks for this." I think it's Chief I'm thanking. He's the only one here. But a bigger thanks rises inside me. "And thank *you*, Jesus." Because it feels like he's in on this too. "Thanks for my best friend, Chief."

When we come out of the woods and onto the plain, all I have to do is whisper, "Gallop, Chief!"

Chief trots first, a rollicking, bouncy trot that makes me laugh. Then he breaks into a gentle canter before running all out. His ears flick up and back, listening for my laughter while keeping an ear out for whatever's ahead. He tosses his head in joy and kicks up his heels, just a bit.

Chief's joy is electric. It passes through my

fingers to every part of my body. I feel as if we're galloping through the sky, above the clouds, leaving every trouble on earth far below.

Chapter 9

Real Friends

At dinner, Dad won't stop talking about his ideas for the pocket hat and an ice scooter. "The ice scooter would be for kids who can't ice skate," he explains. "It wouldn't be a sled. Or skates. Or a scooter. You could sit on it or stand on it, though. I think it would have wheels with tiny spikes that would hold traction on the ice. I'd need to build in brakes, like on a bike. And it would come in seven colors!"

He waves his hands around, trying to help us understand, and he nearly knocks over Lizzy's water glass.

Mom turns to Lizzy. "Why don't you tell Dad about the lizard field trip, honey?"

Lizzy is as excited as Dad when she describes her lizards. Mom says Lizzy can talk as fast as a Quarter Horse runs.

We're almost done eating before I get a word in. I've been thinking about this ever since my wonderful ride on Chief. "Can I take Chief to school with me tomorrow?"

"No," Mom answers. "We've already had this discussion a hundred times."

I knew she'd say no.

"Why would you want to take a horse to school?" Dad asks.

"It would be nice to have a friend there," I answer.

Lizzy gets her teasing look. "You always have Tamson."

"Right," I mutter. "Nope. The truth is, my only real friend is a horse. And he's a friend who can't go to school with me."

"There *is* a friend who can, you know," Lizzy says.

"Yeah." I'm sure she means herself. And she is my friend. "But *you* can't stay in my classroom."

"Not me, silly," Lizzy says.

She can't mean Simon. Not after the way I've treated him.

Mom explains. "Maybe Lizzy means Proverbs 18:24. 'There are "friends" who pretend to be friends, but there is a friend who sticks closer than a brother.'"

Note to self: now I get it. They mean Jesus.

Friday I get up so early it feels like the middle of the night. I make a peanut butter sandwich and fill a plastic bag with carrots, then head for the barn.

Three or four of the horses nicker when I enter the barn. I recognize Chief's friendly greeting. The others are probably saying, "Food? This early? All right!"

But they still have hay, and I don't like to feed Chief before a ride. "Sorry, everybody. Keep munching hay. I'll be back to give you breakfast before long."

The sun still isn't up when I hop from the fence onto Chief's back. There's a touch of chill in the air, just enough to see Chief's breath in tiny clouds. I'm carrying breakfast in the small backpack I always use on breakfast rides and horse picnics. I think this is my favorite time of the day.

Since I want to see the sunrise, we trot up the lane to the best country road in Wyoming. So many trees line the road that it feels like Chief and I are entering a tunnel. After about a mile, I turn Chief down the ditch and up into the Millers' field. Mr. Miller used to have Tennessee Walking Horses. But when his wife got sick, he sold all of them. Now the pasture stands empty. He gave me permission to ride here whenever I like.

For fun, Chief and I canter, circling the pasture until the first light appears above the horizon.

"Time for our picnic, Chief," I tell him.

We stop where I can lean against a tree and face east. I've left Chief's halter on, so I take off his bridle and let him graze close by me.

The sun creeps up—first the top arc, then the golden-red center. And finally, the big ball of a sun hangs low in front of us. Even Chief lifts his head and stares as if he's never seen such a miracle.

"And to think, Chief. This happens every single day."

Halfway through my peanut butter sandwich, I remember the carrots. I fish one out

and hold it for Chief. He chomps half of it in one bite.

"Chief, I've been wanting to talk to you about something." I hold the rest of the carrot in the palm of my hand. He nibbles it between his lips, never letting his teeth touch my fingers. "I owe you a big apology, boy. Yesterday I was a lousy friend, and you know it. I said things to Austin and Tamson about you because, well, because I was a stupidhead. And I didn't stick up for you or for Simon because I wanted Tamson and her friends to be my friends too. And maybe I don't know much about friendship. But I know that you—and Simon—are better friends than they'll ever be."

I already feel better. I always do when I'm with Chief. Maybe that's part of friendship. I take out the rest of the carrots. "So, forgive me?"

Chief steps closer. And before he reaches the

carrots, I blow into his nostrils. He stops, like he's thinking. Then he blows back and snatches up those carrots.

Chapter 10

Stuck Like Glue

Dad drives us to school again. He's already on to a new invention. "Why didn't I think of it before? Why didn't *somebody* think of it before? I'll call it the Spy Shoe, unless I come up with a better name. So easy to make. I'll glue Velcro to the soles of one pair of shoes. Then I'll cut the soles off another pair of shoes and glue the other half of the Velcro on the backs of the soles. The second pair of soles can then be attached to the first pair of shoes so they can be double soled But the trick is—ready for it?"

"Yes!" Lizzy says. "What's the trick?"

"The trick is that the second sole can be affixed backward!"

"Why?" I ask, although I'm only half listening and I don't really want an answer.

"So when you're walking forward, your footprints will look like they're going the other way!" Dad exclaims. "Get it? If someone tries to follow your footprints, they'll just end up farther and farther away from you."

"Genius, Dad! You'll make a fortune," says Lizzy the Encourager. "There's our turn, Dad."

Dad swerves just in time.

Only I wish he'd missed the turn just this once. I've been talking to God inside my head the entire drive to school. But because of all the invention talk, I could use a few more minutes.

I try to finish up fast. *I know you forgive me, Lord. You and Chief always do. And I know there wouldn't even be forgiveness without Jesus. I don't know how to thank you for that. So I'll just say, "Thank you!" every time I tune in today. And please make me a better friend to Simon.*

"You can stop here, Dad," Lizzy says when we're near the loading zone. "Thanks for the ride!"

I pop my seat belt. "Yeah. Thanks, Dad. And I'll look forward to a pair of those Spy Shoes."

Dad's smile takes up his whole face. "They'll come in all sizes, Winnie."

Before we even get out of the car, I hear Tamson shouting, "There he is! The Insect Boy of Prairie Elementary. Go away, Simon! I'll bet you have bugs in your hair!"

Lizzy and I run up and stand beside Simon.
"What's the matter with you, Tamson?" I
demand.

Lizzy and Simon stare at me like *I'm* the one
with bugs in my hair.

Tamson looks even more surprised. But
then she laughs. "What's the matter with *you*,
Winnie?" She pulls an envelope from her pocket. "Okay. Capri got sick and can't come to my
party. Landri said you might as well come in
her place." She hands me the envelope. "Here.
This should put you in a good mood."

I stare down at the invitation to Tamson's
sleepover party. I've wanted this so much. I've
even dreamed about it. *God, help me do the
right thing.*

"Well?" Tamson says. "Aren't you going to
open it?"

I look at Simon. He runs his fingers through

his hair, as if Tamson's right and there really are bugs in it. There aren't, of course. So why would she say that?

"Winnie?" Tamson pokes at the invitation I'm holding. "Didn't you hear me? I said, 'Aren't you going to open it?'"

"Nope." I hand it back. "Thanks, but no thanks."

"What?" Tamson looks like she's going to faint. "Wh-why not?"

"I already have plans . . . to hang out with friends."

I turn to Simon. "Simon, do you want to come over and ride Chief after school?"

Simon's eyes are as big as Chief's. "Me? Why do you want *me* to ride with you?"

I finish his rhyme: "Because I have a Friend who sticks like glue."

Chapter 11

Here, There, and Everywhere

Simon, Lizzy, and I take the bus together after school. From our seat in the back, we can hear Tamson and the sleepover party girls laughing. But we're laughing too. And I think our laughter is better because it's 100 percent friendly.

It's not until we're off the bus and walking

down the lane to our ranch that I think to ask Simon, "You've ridden horses before, right?"

Simon takes a minute to answer. "Austin is the twin with horse. He won't let *me* ride, of course."

"You're kidding!" Lizzy says. "That's so unfair. I know you like horses. Won't your dad get you a horse too?"

Simon shrugs.

I get the feeling there's more to this story.

Lizzy shakes her head. "You're not afraid like me, are you?"

"Not afraid to ride a horse." He grins at me. "If I have your help, of course."

Lizzy watches at the gate while Chief sidles up to the fence to let us mount.

"Uh, aren't you forgetting something, Winnie?" Simon asks.

I'm starting to realize that sometimes Simon doesn't rhyme when he's feeling nervous, or sad, or scared. I'm not sure what he's feeling right now. But I send off a quick prayer that God will help him enjoy this ride. "Simon, we don't need a saddle. Chief is so gentle and so soft. You'll think you're sitting on a pillow."

"Austin never rides bareback," he says. "Royal Princess might attack."

Not a great rhyme. But it was still a rhyme. Simon must be feeling better already. He's on the top rung of the fence with me.

I scratch Chief's jaw to thank him for standing so still. Then I climb on and scoot up to his withers. "Your turn, Simon. Slip on behind me. You can hold onto my waist as tight as you want."

"You can do it, Simon!" Lizzy sounds like a cheerleader.

Simon lowers himself onto Chief and grabs me around the waist.

"See?" I say. "Isn't Chief comfortable?"

He's scooched so close to me I can feel his head nodding.

"Have fun!" Lizzy says. She waves at us.

I move Chief into a slow walk, and Simon's

grip tightens so that it's hard to breathe.
"We'll just walk as long as you want to,
Simon." I guide Chief to the lane. We plod
along in silence for a couple of minutes, and
I feel Simon's grip relax a little.

"Can you smell horse? And pines? And
maybe the promise of rain in the air?" I stroke
Chief's neck with one hand.

"And the breeze," Simon says. "Winnie,
please?"

I'm afraid he's going to ask me to go
back. Maybe he didn't really want to ride,
and I've made him do it. "Please what,
Simon?"

"Go faster?" he answers.

Yes! I urge Chief into a gentle lope, his
smoothest gait. When I'm sure Simon is all in,
I give Chief the signal to gallop. "Hang on,
cowboy!"

Simon laughs. "This is amazing! I never knew. Chief is a great friend. And Winnie is too."

The wind dries my happy tears before they reach my cheeks. We are four friends on a ride I won't ever forget: Simon, Chief, me, and Jesus. I know Jesus is here with us. Not just because I feel him in the sound of hooves beating, or the sight of the sun peeking through the clouds, or the jiggling of a friend's laughter. He's here because he's a Friend who goes everywhere with me.

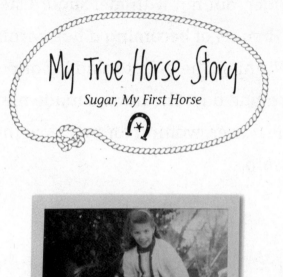

My True Horse Story

Sugar, My First Horse

Good ol' Sugar was my first best friend. Dad led me on Sugar when I was two, and I rode by myself at three, thanks to Sugar's sensitive nature. She might try to run with an

older rider, but not with me. Sugar listened
to my dreams of becoming a horse trainer
(like Winnie). She didn't mind if I griped
about a bad day. She always made me feel
like she'd been waiting for me. Now that's
friendship.

Top Five Lessons I Learned from Sugar

1. Sometimes the best thing a friend can do is listen.
2. It's a great gift to let people believe you're really glad to see them . . . even if you don't feel that way at first.
3. Love can be sacrificial—like carrying someone to a place she'd like to go instead of going where *you* want.
4. Take the time to really get to know a friend.
5. When you fall off, get right back on.

Bonus lesson: God created an amazing animal in the horse. Imagine coming up with a design for such a beautiful creature—one that's soft, but strong; giving and kind; with a nicker and neigh, two of the best sounds on earth; and the best smell in the entire world! It will be awesome to see Sugar again in heaven.

Fun Horse Facts

- In a gallop, there's a moment when all four of a horse's legs are off the ground at the same time.

- Horses don't need much sleep. They might get 3 to 4 hours a day, but even that sleep doesn't happen all at once. They generally catnap, dozing 10 to 15 minutes at a time. Horses can sleep standing up because of the way their joints lock in place, keeping them from falling down. But some horses will also sleep lying down if they feel secure. Horses in a herd will never all lie

down at the same time—at least one horse
will stay on its feet as a lookout.

- Horses can't vomit because their stomachs
aren't designed to do that. That can be a
big problem, because if a horse eats something bad, like poison, the poison stays
in its stomach. Colic is intense stomach
pain and the leading cause of death in
horses. If you see a horse acting strangely,
kicking its belly, twisting on the ground,
or refusing to eat or drink, it's time to call
the vet.

- You can tell if a horse is cold by feeling
behind its ears. If those spots feel cold,
you can bet that your horse is chilly.

- A mule is a cross between a male donkey
(called a jack) and a female horse (a mare).

Male mules are called johns, and females are mollies.

- A cross between a male horse (a stallion) and a female donkey (a jenny) is called a hinny.

- A zebroid is a cross between a zebra and a horse. A zonkey is a cross between a horse and a donkey.

- Horses have big hearts! The average horse's heart weighs about 9 or 10 pounds. The average human heart doesn't even weigh 1 pound. A man's heart weighs about 10 ounces, and a woman's heart between 8 and 9 ounces.

- Horses have better senses of smell and hearing than humans. With 16 muscles in each ear, a horse can turn its ears in different directions—up to halfway around—to help capture sounds or to check out what's going on in front and behind them.

- If a full-grown horse is under 14.2 (14 hands 2 inches or 4 feet 10 inches), it's considered a pony. Ponies have thicker manes and tails than horses. Some common pony breeds are Connemara, Chincoteague, Icelandic, Shetland, and Welsh Cob.

Horse Terms

Foal—A newborn or very young horse, male or female.

Filly—A young female horse up to four years old.

Horse Colt (or colt)—A young male horse up to four years old. The word *colt* is sometimes used casually to refer to any young horse, male or female.

Yearling—A year-old filly or colt.

Mare—A mature female horse, usually age five or older.

Broodmare—A mare used only for breeding (having foals).

Stallion—A male horse that hasn't had the gelding's surgery. Can be a foal's dad.

Gelding—A male horse that has been gelded (fixed) so he can't mate or be a dad.

Dam—The female parent of a foal (the mom).

Sire—The male parent of a foal (the dad).

Draft Horse Breeds

In this book, Chief is a draft horse, also called a farm horse or a heavy horse. Draft horses are strong and powerful. They can pull plows, cart heavy loads, or take you for long rides. A draft horse is usually between 17 and 18 hands (around 6 feet) high at the withers (shoulder). That's big! But draft horses are born gentle and remain calm, even when things get crazy.

Here are some of the most common breeds of draft horse:

Belgian—These are huge, muscular horses with kind eyes and good natures. Some farmers still use Belgian draft horses to pull plows and work in the fields. A Belgian horse can weigh up to a ton (2,000 pounds), which makes it about as heavy as a black rhinoceros!

Clydesdale—These are big, beautiful, brown horses with white feathered legs (long, fluffy fetlocks that can go up to the knee). Clydesdales have wide nostrils, big ears, and lovely, kind eyes. Although they started out as farm workers, now most people use these trustworthy horses for riding or showing.

Haflinger—This smaller version of a work horse is only 14 hands high (under 5 feet), but Haflingers are so strong and sure-footed that they were perfect for carrying large packs in the mountains. Some Austrian farmers still use them to carry hay, but most people today use Haflingers for riding or in harness. These hardworking, calm horses can live to be 40 years old!

Percheron—Unlike the brown and reddish Clydesdale and Belgian horses, Percherons are black or gray. In the Middle Ages, they were used as war horses. Today, still strong, intelligent, and good natured, Percherons may show up as draft horses to pull plows and haul loads. But most people love riding and showing this gentle but lively horse.

Shire—Shires are the biggest of the draft horses, weighing over a ton and standing up to 18 hands tall. Picture a knight in full armor riding a beautiful black horse into battle—that's a Shire. Because of their high-stepping gait and their graceful, aristocratic beauty, Shires no longer work in fields or pull heavy loads. Their owners prefer to ride and show their gentle and kind friends.

Parts of the Horse

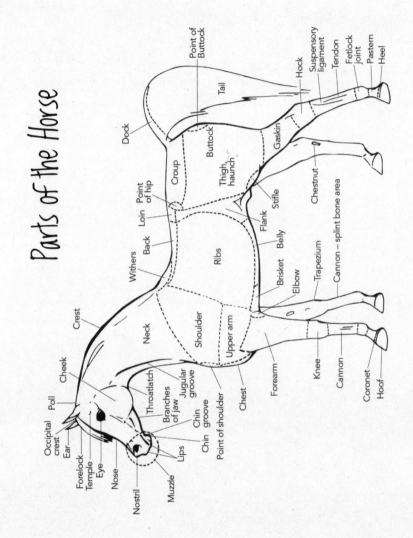

About the Author

Dandi Daley Mackall is the award-winning author of about 500 books for children and adults. She visits countless schools, conducts writing assemblies and workshops across the United States, and presents keynote addresses at conferences and events for young authors. She is also a frequent guest on radio talk shows and has made dozens of appearances on TV. She has won several awards for her writing, including the Helen Keating Ott Award for Outstanding Contribution to Children's Literature and the Edgar Award, and is a two-time winner of the Christian Book Award and the Mom's Choice Award.

Dandi writes from rural Ohio, where she lives with her husband, surrounded by their three children, four granddaughters, and a host of animals. Visit her at www.DandiBooks.com and www.facebook.com/dandi.mackall.

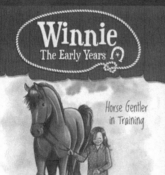

S★T★A★R★L★I★G★H★T

Animal Rescue

More than just animals need rescuing in this series. Starlight Animal Rescue is where problem horses are trained and loved, where abandoned dogs become heroes, where stray cats become loyal companions—and where people with nowhere to fit in find a place to belong.

#1 Runaway

#2 Mad Dog

#3 Wild Cat

#4 Dark Horse

Read all four to discover how a group of teens cope with life and disappointment.

WWW.TYNDALEKIDS.COM